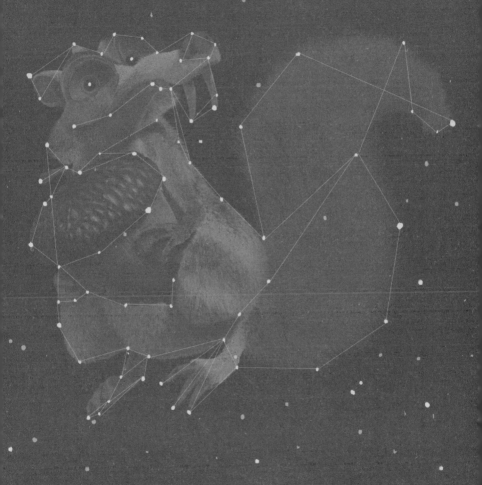

A division of Bonnier Publishing
853 Broadway, New York, New York 10003
Copyright © Ice Age: Collision Course TM & © 2016 Twentieth Century Fox Film Corporation. All Rights Reserved.

SIZZLE PRESS is a trademark of Bonnier Publishing Group, and associated colophon is a trademark of Bonnier Publishing Group.
Manufactured in the United States BRR0516
First Edition 10 9 8 7 6 5 4 3 2 1

sizzlepressbooks.com
bonnierpublishing.com

# THE JUNIOR NOVEL

A division of Bonnier Publishing

New York, New York

# MEET THE
# ICE AGE GANG!

# MANNY

Manny the mammoth is the loving husband to Ellie and is always ready to help out, even when times get tough.

# ELLIE

With a heart almost as big as she is, Ellie is the caring wife to Manny and the protective mother of Peaches.

# PEACHES

This fun-loving, adventurous mammoth is daughter to Manny and Ellie. She's been busy planning a wedding to her fiancé Julian, all while trying to save the planet.

# JULIAN

This easygoing mammoth is Peaches fiancé and is just trying to get Manny to accept him into the family.

# SCRAT

This prehistoric squirrel is always searching for a place to bury his beloved acorn. His hunt has certainly caused some serious problems in the past, and now it's no different! He has accidentally launched an asteroid that's on a collision course with Earth.

# SID

This high-energy but goofy sloth always has a can-do attitude. Even the possibility of the world ending won't stop his search for love.

# BUCK

This one-eyed weasel finds a way to save the world from disaster, but can he find a way to make his plan work?

# DIEGO AND SHIRA

These sabre-toothed tigers are tough adventurers and helpful friends to the Ice Age group, no matter what challenge lies ahead of them.

# CRASH AND EDDIE

The adopted brothers of Ellie, Crash and Eddie are twin possum brothers who love adventure. They are always getting themselves into trouble—to the dismay of the herd.

# GRANNY

Old but tough, Sid's Granny is an elderly sloth who is sharp-tongued and always says what she's feeling.

# BROOKE

New to the Ice Age gang, this sloth loves her crystals and is an enthusiastic Geotopia tour guide for the prehistoric pals. She also has a serious crush on Sid.

# SHANGRI-LLAMA

This yoga-obsessed leader of Geotopia has only crystals and Zen on his mind. His endless ways to stretch and contort his body are always sure to bring laughter to the group.

# TEDDY

This bunny is all about fitness and health—and staying young forever. His high level of energy is very contagious!

# GAVIN, ROGER, AND GERTIE

These three are a family of flying dinosaurs who are determined to stop Buck and his mission to save the world. But are they friend or foe? Only time will tell!

# PROLOGUE

A SQUIRRELY LITTLE CRITTER called Scrat scampered across a vast glacier, carrying an acorn in his mouth. Acorns were his favorite things, and he would go to the ends of the earth to keep them safe. He stopped in the middle of an ice field, glancing around with his bugged-out eyes. Nobody was nearby. It seemed like a great place to store his nut. He dug in a frenzy.

The ice broke under him. Scrat fell, squealing as he tumbled deep inside a narrow opening. He dropped for a long time, passing through hundreds of years of layers of ice. Scrat was startled as he saw strange creatures embedded in the ice.

The acorn landed in an open metallic area and bounced around. Scrat thumped down on the metal floor and scrambled to catch his nut. He was in the command center of a spaceship that had been frozen in the ice for eons.

After another wild bounce, the acorn wedged behind the flying saucer's joystick.

Scrat yanked on his stuck nut. The joystick clicked into gear. The spaceship launched upward, shearing through the layers of ice and blasting out of the glacier. He screeched as the spaceship zoomed through Earth's atmosphere and into the solar system beyond.

Scrat wiggled the joystick, squeaking as he steered the vessel wildly. He ping-ponged the spaceship into a bunch of asteroids, pushing them in a new direction. The asteroids—many smaller and medium-size ones, followed by one gargantuan space rock—now hurtled toward Earth. . . .

# CHAPTER ONE

IN A SUNNY, SNOWY VALLEY, two mammoths played hockey on a frozen lake. Using his trunk, the larger mammoth swiped his stick, sweeping an empty turtle shell along the ice.

Two possums named Crash and Eddie commented on the hockey match using pinecones as microphones.

"It's a beautiful day out here on the ice," announced Crash, "as father meets daughter in a quest for hockey supremacy."

"It's Manny meets Peaches," said Eddie.

Crash nodded. "Mammoth meets mammoth."

Manny narrowed his eyes as he skated toward his young adult daughter.

Peaches hunkered down in front of the goal, prepared to protect the net.

Manny gave his own play-by-play of his moves as he sped up. "The blazing mammoth takes it on the breakaway. There's never been a player so tough, so graceful—"

"So destined to lose," finished Peaches.

"He fakes right," continued Manny, flipping the turtle puck. "He fakes left."

"Fooling no one but himself," Peaches said, laughing. She darted out her stick, and stole the puck from her father. "What's wrong? Lose something?"

She skated past Manny, forcing him back on defense. He moved in front of the goal, blocking the net with his bulk.

Peaches grinned, expertly spinning the turtle shell on the end of her hockey stick.

"Okay, Fuzzball," said Manny. "Let's see what you got."

"You asked for it," Peaches replied. She took off toward her father, stickhandling the puck. When she got close, Peaches skidded to a halt, spraying Manny with shaved ice.

He gasped and rubbed his eyes.

Peaches smacked the puck, and the shell spun past Manny's feet into the net.

"Yes!" Peaches shouted, gloating. "She dominates. Again."

Manny groaned. "Oh, please, I went easy on you. That's called good parenting."

"Yeah, right," replied Peaches. "Face it; I rule the ice now."

Manny put his trunk around his daughter's shoulders. "Oh, you talk a big game, hotshot. All right, how about best of three?"

"Woo-hoo!" someone with a goofy male voice cheered. "Yes! Touchdown!"

Manny winced as he saw his daughter's fiancé, Julian, stepping awkwardly onto the ice. There was nothing really *wrong* with him, but his upbeat, enthusiastic personality got on Manny's nerves.

"Wait, no," said Julian. "That's not right.

Not touchdown. What is it? Hole in one?" He slipped across the ice, bumping into Manny. "Oh, sorry!"

Peaches grinned at her future husband. "Julian, you saw me score!" she said.

"You were amazing," Julian replied. His feet slid out from under him.

Peaches caught him. "Careful."

"The ice is really . . . icy," said Julian. Peaches helped him slide toward the shore. "It's like supersize extra value icy. But I'm getting better, right?"

Manny watched his daughter leave with

her fiancé. The two young mammoths were obviously deeply in love, but Manny couldn't help feeling that he was losing his daughter too soon. "Okay," he said with a sigh. "We'll play . . . later."

His wife, Ellie, and Sid the sloth's grandmother joined Manny as he trudged off the ice.

"So she whupped your butt again, huh?" Ellie teased.

"With a butt that size," added Granny, "that's a whole lot of whupping."

"There was no whupping," Manny

protested. "Just a loving father sharing some strategy with his only daughter."

Peaches and Julian circled back. Julian now held a bunch of wildflowers in his trunk. He gave them to Ellie. "For you, my mom-in-law-to-be," he said. "Buttercups. Nature's sunshine."

"Isn't 'sunshine' nature's sunshine—?" asked Manny.

Ellie silenced him with a jab. "Aw, thank you, Julian," she said. "It's been so long since anyone's given me flowers, but you don't have to bring us presents."

"But it makes me happy," replied Julian.

Manny started to roll his eyes, but Julian looked at him, so he squinted.

"And for you, my guru, my rock, my main mammoth," Julian told Manny, "to you I give the greatest gift of all." He stretched out his trunk and stepped closer to Manny.

Manny recoiled. "Wait. What are you doing?"

"Come on, Bro-Dad," said Julian, patting his chest. "Bring it in." He reared up on his hind legs, clinching Manny in a bear hug.

Manny froze inside the embrace. He

couldn't remember ever feeling so awkward.

"I can feel your heart beating," Julian said.

"Okay," said Manny, squirming free. "That's enough of that."

"You'd better get used to it," Ellie whispered. "They'll be living right next door."

Peaches nudged Julian with her shoulder. "C'mon; want to go?"

Ellie cleared her throat. "Actually," she said in an exaggerated tone, "weren't you going to help me—with *the thing*?"

Peaches nodded. "Right. Got to do *the thing*."

"I can do the thing," Manny offered.

"No," Ellie and Peaches said together.

Peaches shrugged. "It's a girl thing."

Ellie patted Manny's cheek with her trunk. "Hey, why don't you go do a guy thing? You don't spend nearly enough time with your friends."

"I don't?" Manny asked.

"I'll see you later," replied Ellie, already walking away with Peaches. She winked, and added, "On this special day." Then she giggled and wiggled her butt as she sauntered away.

"Uh," said Manny. "Okay."

# CHAPTER TWO

ELLIE'S SUGGESTION SEEMED like a good idea. So Manny met one of his closest buddies, a sabre-toothed tiger named Diego, at the local watering hole.

Small, portly animals called hyraxes served them fruity drinks.

"Women," Manny complained to Diego.

"Yeah, women," agreed Diego. "Um . . . what about them?"

"I don't get them," replied Manny. "Like Ellie. Life's great with her. There are no surprises, and nothing ever happens. But then today . . . she giggled. Does Shira ever giggle?"

Diego glanced to the side, where a female sabre-toothed tiger snarled ferociously as she chased an antelope. "Shira's not a big giggler," said Diego.

"Well, Ellie giggled," said Manny, confused. "And then she wiggled. I have no idea why she could be acting so weird."

"Women," Diego replied.

"Women," agreed Manny.

"Women!" one of the hyraxes squeaked. He dropped a tiny umbrella into Manny's drink.

A crash echoed across the watering hole. "Hello?" their friend Sid called from a distance.

"Speaking of weird . . . ," whispered Diego.

Sid staggered over. The sloth was a disaster, and looked trampled. His eyes were swollen shut. "Anybody there?" cried Sid with his arms outstretched. "Marco? Polo?" He bumped into Manny's giant butt. "Oh, hi, Manny." He waved his hand in front of his nose. "Whew, your breath is awful."

"What happened to you?" asked Diego.

"Oh, nothing," Sid fibbed. "Everything's great!"

"Okay, let me guess," said Diego. "Your girlfriend, Francine, dumped you."

Sid's lower lip quivered. "And then there was an incident with poison ivy." He burst out into sobs. "What is wrong with me? Everybody has somebody, and all I've got is my boyish good looks!" He wiped his eyes with poison ivy leaves. "So . . . itchy," he groaned.

Manny slapped the poison ivy out of Sid's claws. "Let's get you cleaned up." The mammoth led the way back to the valley.

When they reached the spot where Manny usually slept with his family, Diego stopped short, peering around suspiciously. The valley was dark and empty. "Why is it so quiet?" he asked.

"Because the world is mourning my loss," sobbed Sid.

Manny's eyes grew wide as he searched for his wife and daughter. "Ellie? Peaches?" he called. "Where is everyone?"

Animals jumped out from behind trees. "Surprise!" they shouted, throwing streamers that landed on Manny's head.

Ellie smiled. She looked particularly beautiful as she nuzzled up beside him.

Nearby, Crash and Eddie yanked down a cloak of leaves, revealing an ice sculpture of Ellie and Manny.

"Happy anniversary, honey," Ellie whispered in Manny's ear.

Manny gulped. "Anniversary?" He had totally forgotten. "Oh! *That's* the thing."

Ellie softly giggled and wiggled again,

bumping into Manny playfully.

"Now it's your turn, Bro-Dad," said Julian.

"Yeah, we want to see what you got Ellie," added Crash.

"Manny," Eddie chanted, pumping his arms. "Manny!"

Crash and all the other animals picked up the chant until everyone cheered his name.

Manny shifted his feet.

The crowd fell silent, staring at him.

Manny blinked at them.

"He forgot," a nearby animal said.

Ellic glanced sideways at Manny, and he

felt heartbroken at how disappointed she looked. "Ellie, I—" He tried to apologize. "I—"

A bone-shaking explosion echoed in the sky. Everyone looked up. The atmosphere erupted with shooting stars. The animals oohed and aahed at the gorgeous display.

"He didn't forget," said a hefty glyptodon. "That's how big Manny's love is for her."

Another meteor illuminated the night with fiery colors. Ellie smiled at Manny. "I was so afraid you'd forgotten, but you lit up the sky for me. How did you do it?"

"Uh, well . . . ," Manny said. "I . . . um . . . A

magician never reveals his secrets."

"Aw," Ellie said with a sigh. "Thank you."

Friends handed them coconut drinks, and they sipped together, basking in their love.

Peaches bumped into her father. "Wow, Dad. Best present ever," she said as she crunched into an apple.

"You, sir," Julian told Manny, "are an education in marital excellence." He wrapped his trunk around Manny and Ellie. "I'm really going to miss you guys when we leave."

Manny spat out his drink.

Peaches choked on her apple, then

coughed it out. A chunk hit Manny in the eye.

"Uh, actually . . ," she said to Julian, "I hadn't told them yet."

"Oh," said Julian. He grinned at his future in-laws. "Surprise?" Seeing their horrified looks, Julian shuffled away to the buffet.

Manny fixed Peaches with a stare. "You're leaving?" he asked.

"I thought you guys were going to live with us for the first couple of years," said Ellie.

"I know," Peaches replied, "but Julian and I want to roam for a while."

Returning from the buffet, Julian added,

"Yeah, travel, explore, just go wherever. No plan is the best plan; that's my philosophy."

"That's not a plan," countered Manny. "Or a philosophy. Or very safe."

"Dad, we're young," argued Peaches. "We can worry about being safe when we're old and boring . . . like you and Mom."

Julian put his trunk around Peaches. "I think we should just—"

"Excuse me," Manny interrupted harshly, "this is a family discussion."

Julian quickly slid his trunk off of Peaches. "But aren't I part of your family?" he asked.

"Not yet, you're not," Manny replied, visibly irritated.

Diego stepped into the middle of the discussion. "We have a problem," he said.

"Not now," said Manny. "*I* have a problem."

"This one's bigger," said Diego. He turned the mammoth's head up to the sky over Ellie's shoulder.

A flaming meteorite whooshed down. Manny stumbled backward in shock.

Ellie asked, "Manny?"

Manny shook his head to clear his panic. "Uh . . . okay!" he called out. "Party's over, everyone! Have a good night. And leave right now!" He grabbed coconut drinks out of guests' paws, pushing them away.

"What are you talking about?" asked Ellie. She hadn't yet seen the meteorite. "The party just got started."

Manny let out a big fake yawn. "Yeah," he said, "I'm getting kind of sleepy." He steered Ellie toward shelter. "We should go."

Ellie struggled away from him. "What's gotten into you?" Then she spotted the other animals staring upward. She and Peaches both turned to see the meteorite zooming overhead.

Its flames brightened the ground as it passed. With a giant explosion, the meteorite slammed into the cliff alongside the valley. The animals screamed and stumbled as the ground shook from the blast.

An aardvark pointed up. "Look, more are coming!" he screamed. "It's a meteor shower!"

# CHAPTER THREE

**"METEOR?" EDDIE GASPED.**

Crash sniffed his own armpit. "Shower?"
The possums clung to each another, shaking
in fear.

"Manny's love is killing us!" a horselike
creature screamed as it galloped by.

Ellie glared at her husband. "This is all part
of your magic show?"

A meteorite splintered a tree nearby, but Manny shrugged it off. He was more afraid of his wife's realization that he'd forgotten their anniversary. "Abracadabra?" he said sheepishly.

Peaches shoved between them. "Can you guys deal with this later?"

"Come on," Diego urged the mammoths. "We need to take cover."

The group took off running as meteorites streaked overhead, some blasting into trees around them. Other animals raced by, yelping in terror. A rumbling thump made Manny glance behind him as he ran. A meteorite had crashed down and rolled after his family, knocking trees down on either side. They stopped at the edge of the frozen lake.

"Everyone, jump!" Manny shouted.

The friends belly flopped onto the lake, sliding onto the ice.

The meteorite rolled up a chute on the frozen shore, launching overhead. Then the fiery boulder slammed down in front of the friends, shattering the ice.

Manny scrambled to avoid the ragged hole. He slipped around it, pushing Ellie to a safer spot. They needed to find shelter! He spotted a hollow in the rocks. "The cave!" he hollered, running toward it while herding his friends and family with his tusks. "Get inside. Move!"

The group huddled together in their stone bunker as the meteorites exploded outside.

A close blast shuddered the rock floor. Peaches screamed.

"It's okay, sweetheart," said Manny. He reached for her with his trunk, but Peaches was already holding on to Julian.

Sid tiptoed toward the cave exit and peeked at the sky. "Hey, it sounds like it's slowing down." He stuck his whole head outside.

"Yup, it's definitely over," he said.

But then a meteorite as big as Peaches walloped the ground.

Sid turned toward his friends. The meteorite had burned a stripe of fur off his chest. "Okay. one," he said.

To be safe, the rest of the group waited until dawn and then emerged from the cave. The meteorites had blasted and warped the landscape. Wide craters smoked, gaping in the ice. Manny and his friends walked through the wreckage, stunned at the impressive devastation.

A loud growl from one crater made Manny

step back. "Uh . . . hello?" he called out.

Something panted as it crawled out of the

pit. Manny and his family backed away. The

smoke cleared, revealing a one-eyed weasel

standing on the pit's rim.

"Hello, mammals," he said.

Crash and Eddie slid down Manny's tusks,

cheering.

"Hi, Buck!" Eddie greeted their old friend.

The herd had met Buckminster when they

traveled to the lost Dinosaur World. Buck

was a little nutty—he had once married a

pineapple!—but he was loyal and brave.

Buck disappeared back into the crater as he tried to drag a stone tablet onto the surface.

"Bye, Buck," said Crash.

"A little help here, please?" Buck said, struggling under the weight of the tablet.

Manny snagged both Buck and his tablet, and dropped them onto flat land.

"Hey, Buck," said Diego. "Welcome back, buddy."

"This is Buck?" asked Shira. "The dinosaur whisperer?"

Buck shook Shira's paw. "I have one eye but

all my original teeth." He opened his mouth. "Would you like to count them?"

Shira recoiled. "No, thank you."

Buck launched into cartwheels. He passed Julian and stopped under Peaches, smiling up at the teen mammoth. "This must be . . . Nectarine."

"Peaches," said Peaches.

"I am deeply honored," replied Buck.

"Sweet eye patch," Julian told the weasel. "Very gangsta."

Buck smiled. "Thank you." He pointed a paw at Julian. "I like this kid."

"What are you doing here?" growled Manny.

Buck leaped up on a tree stump. "Well, I—" he began, then halted, as if listening to the stump. "What?" he asked the blasted tree. "I'm trying. But how do you tell someone they're doomed?" He looked up at the other animals. "He's stumped. Ha."

"We're not doomed," argued Manny. "It was just a meteor shower. The show's over."

Buck hopped onto Manny's head. "Quite the contrary, old chap," he said. "It's just the beginning." He pointed at the tablet he dragged out of the underworld. "I found a prophecy. Everything on this tablet comes true. See for yourselves."

The animals peered at the markings.

"Every hundred million years or so," Buck explained, translating the story being told in the ancient scratches on the tablet, "the world gets a cosmic cleansing. Before the dinosaurs, there were these horseshoe crab–looking things. Then a meteorite hit. *Boom!* Bye-bye. Next came the dinosaurs. Meteorite. *Boom!* Bye-bye. And coming up next . . . mammals. Meteorite. *Boom!* Bye-bye."

Crash giggled. "Stupid mammals."

"That's us," said Eddie.

Crash screamed.

Buck scanned the sky. He pointed to a spot of yellow light in the distance. "There she is. The mother of all asteroids screaming toward us. Not even going underground will save us this time," he said.

Everyone looked terrified.

"No worries," said Buck cheerfully, "because I've got a plan."

"Really?" asked Manny. "You have a plan to stop an *asteroid*?"

# CHAPTER FOUR

"Look," said Buck, pointing

at the tablet. A mountain range loomed around

a crater in the drawing. "The last two asteroids

that have pummeled the earth have landed

in the same spot. It's about to happen again.

We've got to go there and see what's attracting the asteroid. Once we know why it's coming to that spot, we can figure out how to send that space rock somewhere else."

Manny peered down at the drawing. "Even if we get to the crash site," he asked, "how do we change what is literally written in stone?"

"The dinosaurs were wiped off the face of the earth," Buck replied, "but some escaped. They changed their fate, and we can change ours, too. Who's with me?"

Manny gathered his friends in a huddle. "So, what do you think?"

"Honestly, I'm worried the weasel's right," said Ellie.

Diego peeked at Buck, who gave him a thumbs-up. "Buck has saved our lives before, right? Maybe we should trust him," he said.

"Okay," Manny decided. "I guess we're in."

"Excellent," said Buck. "Now we'd better get on the road because time until impact is roughly two days, four hours, one minute, and sixteen seconds."

———————————

Buck led the mammals across the blasted valley. Ellie and Manny followed at the rear of the marching animals.

Manny glared at Julian and Peaches walking together up ahead. "Look at him," he said. "Who walks like that?" He imitated Julian's cheerfully bouncy stride. "Ooh, look at me. I'm Julian," he mocked his future son-in-law. "Give me a hug, Bro-Dad."

Julian glanced back.

Manny stumbled. "Ooh, look at that pretty bird there," he said, but he pointed at a disgusting vulture.

"That *is* a pretty bird," Julian called back. "Good eye, Manny."

When Julian turned around, Manny scowled. "She thinks we're going to let her just stroll into the wilderness with that guy?"

"Stop picking on him," Ellie scolded.

Manny nudged her. "Come on, El; you're not still mad at me, are you?"

"No," Ellie replied, "I am not still mad, because that's not how I want to spend what could be our final days together. But if we survive, you're in for it."

Manny nodded and sighed. "If we survive, we lose our daughter."

"Well . . . ," said Ellie, "I've been thinking

about that too. What if . . . we can convince them to stay near us?"

Manny smiled. "I like it. But how?"

"The way we always do," Ellie replied. "We make her think it's her idea."

Manny hugged his wife. "You sneaky minx," he said.

"Let's just hope we haven't lost our touch," said Ellie.

Buck jumped up on a boulder alongside the convoy. He held up a shard from a meteorite. "Behold, mammals. Fresh from the cosmos." Buck licked the space fragment. "I taste iron, carbon . . . and a hint of nickel. Space tastes lonely." He tossed the rock. It landed near another meteorite shard. Buck's eyes widened when both fragments wiggled . . . and quickly snapped together.

"Hey, look," said Crash, "I found another one." He held up a bigger chunk.

Nearby, Eddie also held a shard of rock. "Me too."

The meteorite fragments jolted toward each another, yanking the possums so they collided in a heap. They struggled to pull the space rocks apart.

"Yours is attracted to *me*," Crash said.

"No," argued Eddie, "it's yours that is attracted to *me*."

More meteorite fragments flew at them. The possums screamed as they were pelted by space rocks.

"Curse our animal magnetism!" cried Eddie.

"Stupendous," said Diego. "Now we have something to play with during our final hours."

"You're missing the point, tiger," Buck said. "They're magnets." He paused and thought for a second. "What if we use those magnets to attract the asteroid somewhere else? As in not toward Earth?" The weasel pointed up at the mega-asteroid in the sky. "If we can launch magnetic crystals into space, they will pull the asteroid off course."

"So we just need to launch a bunch of stuff into space," said Crash. "That's easy, right?" He grabbed two of the magnetic meteorite shards and jammed them into his backpack.

"Do we really need to lug your pet rocks around with us?" asked Diego.

"No," replied Buck, his eye twinkling, "but if we left behind everything heavy and useless, we'd also have to get rid of you."

"Oh!" Crash told Diego. "Get some aloe vera on that . . ."

"Because you got *burnt,* son!" finished Eddie.

Buck wisely stepped away from the sabre-toothed tiger. "Come on, mammals!" he called out, heading along a path between two hills. "This trail will take us directly to the crash site."

The herd followed him out of the valley.

# CHAPTER FIVE

THE MAMMALS TRAILED AFTER
Buck for the rest of the day, crossing streams
and pushing through thick forests. As darkness
fell, they reached another frozen lake at the
edge of the woods.

Buck peered up at the asteroid in the
distance. "Let's stop here for the night."

"Is there time to rest?" asked Manny.

"Well, the asteroid is prominent," replied Buck. "Eminent. And getting more imminent. Fortunately, right now, none of that is pertinent. I'd say yes."

Manny spotted Diego and Julian nearby. The tiger and the young mammoth laughed. They shared a complicated handshake that finished with them wiggling trunk and paws together. Julian headed over to Peaches.

"*Hasta mañana*, J-man," Diego called after him, and bumped into Manny.

"What was that?" Manny demanded.

"What was what?" asked Diego.

Manny imitated Diego and Julian's complicated handshake.

"Oh, that," said Diego. "It's a cool way to peace out. Julian taught it to me."

"What, are you guys buddies now?" asked Manny.

"He's a good kid," Diego replied. "I like his philosophy. Give him a chance. Bond with him."

Manny glared at Julian, who was gathering twigs by the campfire.

"Bonding," Ellie said softly, coming up

beside Manny. "That's a good idea."

Manny remembered her plan to convince Julian and Peaches to stay. "Gotcha," he said, giving his wife a wink. He walked over to Julian, who was now drumming on a stone with sticks. "Hey," he said, "Bro-Kid. . . ."

"Oh, hey, Bro-Dad," replied Julian. "You here to rock out?" He drummed harder.

Manny snatched the sticks out of Julian's trunk. "Instead of that," he said, "how about a game before bedtime?"

Julian grinned. "No way. You want to play a game with me? Wow. What is honored times one thousand? No. Times one *million*? Because whatever that equals is how honored I am."

"So . . . ," said Manny, "is that a yes or . . . ?"

"Yes, that's a yes," replied Julian. "It's the most yes. It's yes with a bunch of *s*'s so it's like . . . *yesssssssssssssssssss*."

"Great," said Manny. "I'll see you on the ice."

---

Diego sat down on the shore near Peaches to watch the hockey match.

Manny skated backward on the frozen lake, showing off his skills. "Happy?" he asked Diego as he swooped by the tiger.

But Diego winced as Julian slid sloppily onto the ice. "Oh boy," Diego groaned.

Julian wobbled over to a makeshift net and did his best to play goalie. But no matter how gently Manny pushed a turtle shell toward him, the puck got past Julian and plopped into the net.

"These pucks go fast," said Julian.

Manny raised his stick, preparing to shoot again. "The key is to focus," he instructed. "Just watch the puck." Then Manny hit the puck as gently as he could, and the shell slid with excruciating slowness toward the younger mammoth.

Julian tapped the puck with his stick, blocking it. "Hey," he said, surprised. "I did it."

Manny smiled at Julian's astonished pleasure. He skated in a circle, coming around to shoot again. "Too bad you and Peaches are moving away," he hinted. "If you stayed, we could do this all the time."

Julian got into an awkward ready position. "Okay, show me the heat," he said loudly. "I'm like a hockey ninja."

Manny zoomed closer, raising his stick.

"Hey, Peaches!" Julian bragged. "You've got a new hockey partner to replace your dad!"

Manny flinched. He slapped the puck— much harder than he intended. The shell flew into the air and smacked Julian in the forehead.

"Ow," Diego said.

Julian crumpled and thumped onto the ice. It cracked underneath his bulk.

"Oh no," groaned Manny.

"Julian!" Peaches shouted as the ice broke open and her fiancé plopped into the frigid water. She ran over, hoisted him out, and helped him to the campfire to dry off. Crash and Eddie worked together and wrung water out of Julian's sopping fur.

On the other side of the campfire, Manny and Diego sat down next to Ellie. Manny sighed. "I didn't mean to do it. It's not my fault the kid has no reflexes."

Peaches stormed over to her father. "How could you do that to him? I thought you liked Julian."

"I *do* like Julian—" protested Manny.

"You don't act like it," said Peaches. "When

you look at him, all you see is an obstacle. Or worse, a *target*. But I see a sweet guy who's trying his hardest to impress you."

Ellie touched her daughter's shoulder with her trunk. "Peaches—"

Peaches shrugged her off. "No," she said. "Just stop. If we survive, I'm still getting married. I'm still leaving home. Whether you're happy for me or not." She strode away from her parents, back toward where Julian shivered on the other side of the fire.

# CHAPTER SIX

"ALL RIGHT, MAMMALS, TIME to get moving!" Buck announced in the morning. He glanced up at the ball of fiery rock overhead. "Now let's not linger on this, but, yes, I read the tablet wrong. The asteroid is a lot closer than I expected."

Everyone shook off sleep, and packed to return to walking toward the landing site.

"Wait a second," said Sid, his voice rising in alarm. "Where's Granny?" He patted the nearby bushes. "Granny!"

"Maybe she wandered off?" suggested Manny.

Peaches glared at her father. "Maybe she got hit in the head with a puck?"

Diego sniffed the spot where Granny had slept. "I've got her scent. Come on."

The herd hurried after Diego. They tracked Granny's scent through the woods until they came to a foggy hilltop. A volcano loomed beside the crater with smoke billowing out of its main vent.

"Whoa," said Shira.

Buck checked his tablet. The vista matched a drawing on it perfectly. "Mammals, we've made it the crash site!" he announced. "If there's a secret to saving the world, it's here."

Sid peered over the rim of the enormous crater. "What about Granny?"

Diego sniffed the rocky ground. He looked worried, and sniffed again. "Nothing," he said.

Manny wrapped his trunk around Sid's

shoulders. "I'm sorry," he said.

Sid sniffled. "Oh, my sweet, malicious granny," he moaned. "Why does it always have to be the old ones who go first—?"

The friends heard a yowling noise echo up from the forest beside the crater.

"I can still hear her sweet shrill voice." Sid sighed. "Shrieking from the afterlife—"

The wail interrupted him again.

"Granny's alive!" Ellie shouted.

"And she's in trouble," Diego added. He leaped to a lower level in the crater, hurrying toward the noise.

It's business as usual, with Crash and Eddie going head-to-head in a hockey match, before the Ice Age friends learn that a huge asteroid is on a collision course with Earth.

What can the prehistoric herd do to stop the asteroid from slamming into their planet?

How did all this trouble begin? Scrat chased his beloved acorn straight into a spaceship and accidentally launched it into space.

Scrat tries to drive the spaceship but hits a wrong button and ends up floating in the air.

Buck arrives on the scene, ready to save the world.

Buck explains to his friends that an ancient
tablet has clues to where the asteroid will hit.

The Ice Age gang put their heads together to come up with a plan to stop the asteroid from hitting their home.

The friends learn that the meteorites they've been finding are highly magnetic when Crash and Eddie can't separate!

Plan in place, the prehistoric gang head out to save Earth.

Before they found out about the planet being in danger, Julian and Peaches were busy planning their wedding.

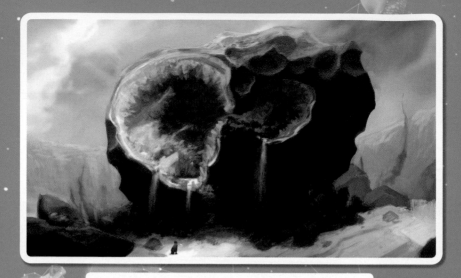

The herd end up at the city of Geotopia,
which is inside a massive geode.

Sid meets a lovely sloth in
Geotopia, and falls hard for her.

The master of Geotopia is the Shangri-Llama and he is always busy doing yoga.

Sid, Manny, and Diego try out some of the Shangri-Llama's fancy yoga moves.

Julian and Manny work together to push a giant crystal into a volcano.

With Earth saved, Julian and Peaches are able to get married with all their friends around.

The rest of the herd followed him down the slope. They rounded a boulder and found Granny lying on a slab in a grassy area sheltered by a wall of hanging vines. A muscular rabbit taller than Sid was giving Granny a thorough massage. He kneaded her loose skin. She yowled in delight.

"Hey!" cried Sid. "Unhand my granny."

"You do," Granny warned the masseur, "and you don't get a tip, Teddy."

"Making you happy is all the payment I need," Teddy replied. He picked her up and carried her through the partition of vines.

"You see?" Granny called back. "This guy gets it."

"Granny—" Sid protested, following the rabbit.

The rest of the group pushed through the hanging vines too. On the other side, they all halted in amazement. A ledge of huge twinkling crystals stretched out from the side of the crater. In the streaming sunshine, the crystals sparkled in every color of the rainbow. A dome of thinner crystals arched over a community in a quartz village. The volcano towered above.

"This is different," said Manny as he looked around in amazement.

A shimmering flash whooshed by his face. The streak slowed until the herd saw that it was actually a young female sloth, riding a crystal hoverboard.

"I can't believe it," the female sloth squealed. "Actual visitors! I sure hope this isn't a—" She stopped talking when she saw Sid, and fell off her hoverboard. "Dream," she finished from the ground.

She clapped twice, and two miniature pink unicorns raced to her side. The female sloth pointed at Sid. The unicorns pushed him toward her. "Hello, handsome," she gushed at him. "I'm Brooke." She patted his face. "Such exquisite bone structure. Such a strong jaw. I'm getting butterflies."

"I'm getting nauseous," groaned Manny.

Buck peered at the hoverboard, and touched the glinting quartz ground and walls of the dome. "This whole place is made of magnetic crystals," he said quietly. "This must be why the meteorites always land here." He sniffed the crystals. "I think the answer to saving the world is right under our noses."

Brooke fluttered her long eyelashes at Sid. "You're here to save the world?"

"I do what I can," Sid replied.

Buck popped up between Sid and Brooke, pointing at the sky. The fiery ball of doom fell closer than ever. "If we don't stop it, that asteroid is going to blow us all to smithereens."

"That is superdisturbing," Teddy said.

"Can you help us?" Buck asked Brooke.

"Global catastrophe isn't really my strong suit," Brooke replied. "You should meet my guru, the Master of Meditation, the Supreme Serene, the Four-Time Heavy Thoughts

Champion of the World, the Shangri-Llama.

He's an awesomely twisty guy, but he's

inventing new mind-expanding yoga poses,

so we'll just let him be. Instead, I'll give you

a tour!"

# CHAPTER SEVEN

THE MINIATURE UNICORNS
tapped their tiny hooves. The slabs of crystals
underneath the herd separated from the ledge,
floating off the ground. Brooke pulled Sid onto
her hoverboard, and she led the group like she
was the conductor on a tram. They glided into
the crystal dome.

Spikes of crystals pointed from the walls, like inside a geode, with the settlement in a chunky cluster on the bottom. Lush, gorgeous plants grew between the pointy spires. All around, animals soared by on floating crystals. Some of the beasts basked in the rainbow sunshine or did yoga on hovering platforms, while others danced with shimmering quartz sticks.

Outside the dome, Manny saw smaller vents glowing with magma along the volcano's steep slopes. He blinked at the crystal paradise. "Where are we?" he asked.

"You're in Geotopia," Brooke replied.

"How long have you lived here?" Ellie asked.

Brooke rubbed her chin. "I've lost track," she said. "A couple hundred years, maybe?"

The rest of the group stared at Brooke. She grinned back at them.

"That's not possible," said Diego.

"Of course it is," replied Teddy. "I'm three hundred and twenty-six years old."

"You don't look a day over two hundred and seventy-five," said Granny.

Shira leaned against Diego. "This place is

magical. It's a giant magnet!"

The crystal tram landed near the dome's edge, and Manny stumbled. "Magical, my—" He yelped as his big butt slid off the side and scraped the spiky ground. A trunk pulled him up. Manny was surprised it was Julian who helped him. "Thanks."

"Pretty wild in here," said Julian.

"Yeah," replied Manny, readjusting himself on the tram.

Julian squirmed uncomfortably. "Manny," he blurted, "you don't like me much—"

"Julian—" Manny interrupted.

"No." Julian kept talking. "It's cool. I'm an acquired taste, but we do have one thing in common." He smiled at Peaches. "We both love her. That's two things if you count having trunks, but you know what I mean."

Manny exhaled. Slowly, he nodded in agreement. Love for his daughter was the most important thing they could possibly share.

# CHAPTER EIGHT

IT WAS GETTING CLOSER.

Much closer. The asteroid's blazing light shimmered inside the dome.

The tram landed on a flat area in the center of Geotopia. Following Julian and Peaches, Manny and Ellie stepped off the platform into a garden between transparent quartz structures.

With the bang of a gong, a fuzzy thing that looked like a bush began to move. A skinny, twisted creature blinked at the herd as it unfolded out of a complicated yoga position. It had red horns and a braided beard.

"Is that a llama?" Granny asked. "I hate llamas. They spit, and they smell!"

"So does she," Diego whispered to Shira.

"Greetings!" the llama said. "The Shangri-Llama will see you now!" He waved a burning stick, spreading stinky incense around himself.

Buck stepped forward. "Nice to meet you,

Your Twistyness," he said. "Lovely home you have here. But . . . there's an asteroid screaming towards us because it's magnetically attracted to your crystals. So, um, we must somehow launch all the pieces of your home into space to pull the asteroid off course. I haven't figured out the launching part yet."

"Nope," replied the Shangri Llama. "Our home keeps us safe." He turned his back on Buck. "Woo! I am bushed." The llama tucked himself into a bush shape and stopped talking.

Buck rubbed his good eye in frustration as he led his friends away from the unhelpful yogi. If only he knew how to shoot the crystals into space, maybe he could convince everyone to help him save all their lives.

As she followed Buck, Peaches rubbed her head affectionately against Julian's.

Manny leaned close to Ellie. "Two days ago," he whispered, "I'd have given anything to keep her with us." He glanced up at the asteroid. "Now I'd give anything to see her get married and leave home."

"Play with her kids," Ellie added. "Dance with her husband."

"Yell at him when he forgets their

anniversary," Manny added.

Ellie smiled, both sad and happy. "It was a good one, wasn't it?" she asked. "Our life? You, me, and Peaches."

"The best," said Manny.

Suddenly the volcano belched out a big smoke ring.

Buck jumped up, screaming in excitement. "Eureka!" He shouted and pointed at the fiery mountain. "That's it! Earth's most powerful propulsive device is right in front of us!"

Everyone stared at the volcano. It looked terrifying, with smoke puffing out and sparks spewing from small vents on its sides. Nobody sane would approach something so dangerous.

"That's our magnet launcher," said Buck.

Diego shook his head. "That's never going to work."

Buck nodded. "It will if we seal the vents around the volcano."

Hot steam spurted from the cracks along the mountain's base.

"That's a crazy plan," said Diego.

"You're a crazy plan," replied Buck.

Diego face-palmed with his paw. "That doesn't make any sense."

Buck jumped on a tall crystal. "Right!" he shouted to everyone. "We need all the crystals loaded into the volcano pronto!"

The Shangri-Llama raised his head. "Nobody do that!" he brayed.

The city creatures glanced around nervously, unsure whose orders to follow.

Brooke stuck two fingers in her mouth and let out a piercing whistle. The citizens snapped to attention. "These crystals are not ours to keep!" announced Brooke. "They came from the sky, and now it's time to give them back."

"Is not!" the Shangri-Llama argued. "Do

you have any idea what will happen to us without those crystals?"

"Change isn't easy," replied Brooke, "but it's part of life."

The creatures all around them murmured agreement.

"It's time to embrace change," said Brooke. She glared at the yoga guru. "Whether you like it or not."

"Not!" the Shangri-Llama snorted.

"Listen, llama," said Brooke firmly. "Either get on board . . . or go twist yourself into a pretzel!" She soared above the city on her hoverboard. "Come on, everybody!" Brooke ordered. "We will help these animals take down our walls, and we will save the world! Grab every crystal you can find!"

Everyone got to work dismantling the shimmering structures.

As Buck organized the animals plugging the smaller vents with the pieces of crystal, Manny hauled a huge woven-vine net of crystals behind him. Other animals passed chunks of quartz paw to paw in a chain all the way up to the top of the volcano.

Halfway up, an exhausted ox stopped

rolling his crystal boulder, wiping his brow.
"Come on!" Granny hollered at him. "Roll
that rock!"

Meanwhile, Julian and hefty animals with
wide tusks pushed a massive crystal up the
slope.

At the top, Brooke oversaw the end of
the chain of creatures who were passing
along smaller crystals. "This is it, friends!"
she cheered. "Down the hatch. Every crystal
counts." The crystals landed in the lava below,
bobbing in the molten rock.

Buck peered into the bubbling crater.

Eventually, the crystals would disintegrate in the lava's awesome heat, but hopefully they would stay solid long enough to do their job. He glanced up at the asteroid. Its impact would wipe out life on Earth. And it was going to happen very soon unless his plan worked.

"We're six minutes behind schedule!" he yelled.

Manny dumped his net of crystals into the lava. "Double time, everyone. We need that big crystal!"

# CHAPTER NINE

**MANNY RUSHED TO HELP JULIAN**

and together they maneuvered the huge crystal.

"Oh, hey, Bro-Dad," Julian greeted him. He sounded exhausted, but he wasn't giving up.

With the help of the other strong-tusked animals, Julian and Manny struggled to shove the crystal boulder across a rock bridge. After that, the other animals' tusks were too wide to fit onto the narrow path, so the mammoths had to push the huge crystal alone.

As they neared the main crater, Manny blocked Julian. "I'll push it in," he insisted. "Go with Peaches and Ellie."

"No," said Julian. "I'm not leaving you. We'll do this together." He wiggled past Manny, and heaved his shoulder against the boulder, pushing it ahead.

Manny joined his efforts. Together they shoved the crystal rock to the lip of the volcano. The ground rumbled as the volcano prepared to erupt. Manny glanced up at the asteroid. It was glowing brighter as it neared Earth's atmosphere.

The crystal boulder was stuck on the high sides of the crater's rim. No matter how hard he and Julian pushed, they couldn't hoist it over the outcropping.

"This isn't working," Manny gasped.

Julian paused, peering over his shoulder at the slope behind them.

"Wait," Julian said, straining to hold the boulder. "I have a plan. Let the crystal go."

Manny squeezed his eyes shut as he pushed. "You know we're trying to get it *in* the volcano, right?"

"I know it sounds crazy," said Julian. "But

. . . trust me. I want to marry your daughter more than anything. I need this to work."

Manny bit his lip. The volcano rumbled again underneath him. Overhead, the asteroid fell ever closer to wiping out life on the whole planet. "Okay," he said. "Let's do it."

Julian nodded. "On my count," he said. "One . . . two . . . *three*!"

Manny and Julian jumped away from the boulder, letting it tumble back down the slope. They galloped after it. The rolling boulder headed for a natural chute in the volcano's rocky side. The chute curved upward, forming a half-pipe. The two mammoths stopped short, watching with wide eyes. The boulder rolled up the curve of the half-pipe, launching into the air, arcing back over Manny and Julian.

Julian closed his eyes, but Manny watched the boulder soar through the sky. It hit the rim of the crater, bounced wildly, and then hit the other side, teetering on the edge.

Julian peeked up at the volcano. "Did it work?"

The crystal boulder fell into the lava.

"Yes!" said Manny. "I take back everything I ever said about you."

Julian grinned, thrilled. Then his smile faltered. "Wait . . . what?"

Manny yanked Julian away from the volcano. "Let's get out of here!" he said.

The volcano rumbled violently as the steam inside it built up to an eruption. Above, the asteroid tumbled ever nearer.

Manny and Julian slid on their big butts down the slope as the volcano's trembling turned to a thunderous shaking earthquake. The two mammoths reached their friends in the dismantled crystal city. Everybody stumbled on the rumbling ground, holding one another as they waited for the eruption, but the shaking and noise ceased.

"What happened?" asked Shira.

Diego shrugged. "Maybe it's the quiet before the crazy?"

The herd stared at the volcano as Granny plugged one last tiny steam vent with her cane.

The earth shook with the loudest roar anyone had ever heard. The volcano erupted upward, spewing out its lava—and the crystals—in a blast of awesome power. Smoke billowed around a central stream of fiery molten rock that stretched all the way into the atmosphere, gushing into space. The lava and crystals spread out in the zero gravity, off to the side of the asteroid. Their combined magnetism shifted the asteroid slowly, pulling it just a few degrees off course.

Down below, the animals held hands as they gaped at the astounding display. Eddie and Crash hugged as the asteroid entered the atmosphere. But the massive meteor skirted Earth, zooming above it and then hurtling away to the other side.

Everyone let out a long, ragged breath. Then they exploded in thunderous cheering.

"We did it!" screamed Manny. "We did it!"

Shira pounced on Diego, tackling him. They rolled around in a happy hug.

Brooke blinked at the sky. "I can't believe it worked." She grabbed Sid, dipped him backward, and planted a kiss on his lips.

"Bring it in, Bro-Son," Manny said, pulling Julian close for a tight hug. "Welcome to the family."

Julian hugged Manny hard, with Peaches and Ellie joining in the love.

After a moment, Manny broke free. He located Buck, and he hoisted the weasel up onto his head. "And you, you coconut," Manny said, "I'll never doubt you again."

The crowd of thrilled animals cheered wildly for Buck.

Buck wiped his tears. "Now I'm crying under the eye patch."

As they celebrated, Sid noticed that the animals from the ruined crystal city were growing old. Brooke's hair turned gray as her face wrinkled up. "Brooke," Sid cried, "what happened?"

"The crystals were keeping us young, Sid," Brooke explained. "We knew this would happen, but the sacrifice was worth it to save Earth."

Sid hugged her tight, trembling with bittersweet tears.

Soon after, Manny and his herd prepared to leave the crystal city. Everyone said fond good-byes. The aged city animals were already rebuilding, using the rubble from the volcano.

"You sure you can't come with us?" Sid asked Brooke.

"Oh, Sidney, I wish I could," Brooke replied. "But we both know this is for the best. You've got your whole life in front of you. Besides, I'll have Granny to keep me company."

Sid gasped, facing his grandmother. "You're staying too?"

"Are you kidding?" said Granny. "This place is great!"

The crystal city citizens were now as old as she was.

"You coming, Gladys?" called Teddy. He stooped over with age, but he was still a hunk.

"What?" shrieked Granny. "I can't hear you."

"What?" Teddy hollered back. "I can't hear you."

As Manny led the herd into the forest, Sid looked back. Granny and Brooke stood together, waving good-bye.

"So long, handsome!" shouted Brooke.

"Bye, Sidney," said Granny.

After the herd walked away, far in the distance, a small meteorite was seen falling from the sky. It landed right into the spring where the animals were sitting. The water sparkled and magically Teddy, Brooke, and the others all turned young again.

# CHAPTER TEN

**THE VALLEY WAS COVERED WITH**

a fresh layer of beautiful snow. It was the day
of Peaches and Julian's wedding. Anyone who
was anyone had come to wish the couple
happiness.

Sid hurried through the crowd, wearing
a twig headset. "Where's the bride?" he
demanded into the wood microphone. "Why
don't I have the bride?"

"Because you're talking into a twig," Diego told him.

The audience gasped in delight as Peaches and Ellie stepped out of the trees, preparing to walk toward the aisle. They both looked beautiful as any mammoths in prehistory. Peaches had a veil of delicate flowers trailing over her face, and Ellie wore a stylish leaf hat.

"I don't know," Peaches said to Ellie. "What am I going to do?"

"Just relax, honey," Ellie said reassuringly. "Deep breaths."

Manny rushed over to his family. He had

a flower corsage pinned to his chest. "What's going on?"

"It's just—" Peaches sighed. "I don't want to leave you guys."

Manny and Ellie shared a significant look.

"Hey, Fuzzball," said Manny softly, "remember the first time that we played hockey? You were so afraid to get on the ice because it was slippery? Remember how I held you up while you started to skate . . . and when I knew you were ready . . . I let you go?"

Peaches leaned against him. "Aw, Dad."

"I know you're ready," Manny told his

daughter. "Now you have to let go."

Ellie adjusted Peaches's veil. "I always knew it would take someone very special to match your spirit. And you found him. Just like I did." She smiled at Manny, but kept speaking to her daughter. "It's your time, sweetie. See the world; chase your dreams."

"Whenever you decide to come back," added Manny, "we'll be here. Okay?"

Peaches swallowed her nerves. "Okay."

The family walked down the aisle, with Crash and Eddie tossing rose petals in front of them. At the altar, Julian waited, smiling so wide. On either side of the aisle, their friends beamed as they watched the two mammoths coming together.

Manny stopped in front of Julian. He took Peaches's trunk with his own and passed it to Julian, who took it tenderly. Ellie and Manny stepped aside, leaving their daughter with the young mammoth who loved her.

The minister was a small hyrax, standing on a pyramid of other hyraxes. He cleared his throat. "Do you, Peaches, take Julian as your husband?" the minister squeaked.

"I do," Peaches said.

The hyrax minister nodded. "Do you, Julian, take Peaches as your wife?"

"Most def," replied Julian.

The minister smiled. "I now pronounce you husband and wife."

The crowd erupted in cheers and applause.

After the ceremony, everyone celebrated with music, dancing, and food. Among their happy friends, Manny and Ellie swayed together on the dance floor, cheek to cheek.

"El," Manny asked, "how about we take a second honeymoon?"

"Where's this coming from?" asked Ellie.

"I was thinking we'd wing it," Manny replied as they danced. "Just hit the road and roam until we find a place we like. No plan is the best plan. That's my philosophy."

Ellie laughed. "No, it's not. But I'm going to hold you to it anyway."

Earth had been saved, and Manny and Ellie were back to a harmonious relationship. All was good with the Ice Age herd.

Don't miss these other
great Ice Age™ books!